anythink

D0923535

MICHAEL DAHL PRESENTS

Dolls of Doom

A TALE OF TERROR BY STEVE BREZENOFF
ILLUSTRATIONS BY MARIANO EPELBAUM

STONE ARCH BOOKS
a capstone imprint

Michael Dahl Presents is published by Stone Arch Books,
A Capstone Imprint
1710 Roe Crest Drive
North Mankato, Minnesota 56003
www.mycapstone.com

Summary: Jasmine has a peculiar fear of dolls. And when her
family goes on vacation to a creepy old hotel, Jas finds that her
room is filled with antique, very real-looking dolls. Each day, the
dolls seem to watch her. Jas tries hard to control her imagination,
but these tiny terrors may turn out to be dolls of doom.

Library of Congress Cataloging-in-Publication Data is available on
the Library of Congress website.

ISBN: 978-1-4965-7342-1 (library hardcover)
ISBN: 978-1-4965-7346-9 (paperback)
ISBN: 978-1-4965-7350-6 (ebook PDF)

Printed in Canada.
PA020

MICHAEL
DAHL
PRESENTS

Michael Dahl has written about werewolves, magicians, and superheroes. He loves funny books, scary books, and mysterious books. Every Michael Dahl Presents book is chosen by Michael himself and written by an author he loves. The books are about favorite subjects like monster aliens, haunted houses, farting pigs, or magical powers that go haywire. Read on!

PEDIOPHOBIA
(PEE-dee-yuh-FOH-bee-uh)

THE FEAR OF
DOLLS

EVERYONE IS AFRAID OF SOMETHING.

I'm afraid of quite a number of things. But a
PHOBIA is a very special fear. It is deep and
strong and long lasting. It is hard to explain why
people have phobias—they just do.

From the first chapter of this book, when Jas
and her family arrive at a weird old hotel and
find a room filled with dolls, I was hooked! Even
though I read it during the day, with sunlight
streaming through the windows, I felt strangely
cold. I was sure that somewhere, where I
couldn't see them, dolls were staring at me with
their glassy, lidless eyes.

Michael Dahl

1

The north shore of Lake Superior was everything to me.

Maybe that's overstating it. Still, my family spent a long weekend there at the end of every summer. It was one last burst of perfection before school for me and my brother, Jason.

That summer, however, was different.

We drove past the Lakeview Inn, where we usually spent our special week. It sat right on the beach in town proper.

This year, though, we couldn't get a room. Dad

tried to book our usual suite, but they said that portion of the inn was being renovated. All the other suites were already reserved.

"It looks fine to me," I said as I looked out the window of Mom's car.

"I'm sure they didn't lie to me, Jas," Dad said, not even looking up from the crossword puzzle on his lap, probably the twentieth one he'd done since we left the house.

Jas was me, of course—short for Jasmine.

"She's right, Dad," Jason said. "I don't see any work being done at all."

"All right, that's enough," Dad said. "I'm sure they're doing work inside. Now let's move on. I'm sure this new place will be just as good."

"Even better," Mom put in as the car sailed right past town. "It's not right in town, so it'll be even more relaxing."

"And there won't be any Wi-Fi, coffee shops, stores, pizza, or doughnuts within walking distance," I added.

"Here it is," Mom said. She turned the car off the big paved two-laner and onto a gravel road that weaved into the woods.

The car bumped and bounced along. Mom seemed to catch every rut, pothole, and massive bump along the trail.

"This can't be right," I said. "Are you sure this isn't some creepy old hunter's driveway?"

Dad had his phone out and was looking through his vacation notes. "The man on the phone said it was really out of the way," he said. "Though he didn't mention off-roading. . . ."

"This is how they live up here, kids," Mom said. She clicked the car into four-wheel drive. "I bet this road is closed six months out of the year too."

"It ought to be closed all twelve," Jason said.

I laughed.

Mom slowly turned through one more curve. The lake came into view. It glittered in the afternoon sun like it was made of frosted glass.

"It's so beautiful," I said, in awe.

"Most beautiful sight in the world," Dad said. He turned around and smiled at me. I had to admit it was good to be back, even at the wrong inn.

Even with a name like . . .

"Devil's Mooring," Mom said as she pulled into the gravel parking lot. "Here we are."

We climbed out. I stood there staring at the inn. It was two stories, and the front was an ornate A-frame. Or it was ornate at one time. By the time my family got there, the paint had peeled and faded, the wood had rotted, and some of the letters above the door had worn away.

All I could make out of the old sign was *come to Devil's ring.*

2

Dad handed me my duffel bag. "In we go!" he said, far too cheery for the setting.

Jason rolled his eyes at me, and we followed Mom and Dad inside.

The lobby was dark and dusty. A man stood behind the counter as if he'd been there forever, watching the door and waiting for us.

"Good afternoon." His voice was as dusty as the lobby. His hair—ragged and gray—hung just past his ears. He wore a high collar, like someone from an old painting, and a fancy-looking suit.

"Hi!" Mom called back as we crossed the big lobby.

We got closer, and I saw now his sunken cheeks, the frizzled ends of his hair, the tattered cloth of his collar, and the wrinkles in his suit.

"I trust you had a pleasant drive?" he said.

My dad opened his mouth to reply, but he never got the chance.

"Please follow me," the old man said. He came out from behind the counter and walked on long, lean legs down the hall. Though his stride was slow, he covered a lot of distance. Even Jason had to hurry to keep up.

"I was so pleased," he said casually as we hurried alongside him, "to hear a family would be staying with us to close out the season."

"Oh?" Mom said. "Are we the only family staying here right now?"

Dad grabbed my hand and gave it a reassuring squeeze.

"I'd have to check the registry, madame," the man replied as he turned a corner.

Ahead, the sconces flickered in the wide, red-carpeted hallway. An intricate pattern of yellow and purple and teal zigzagged along the carpeting.

Down the center, it was faded from years of being walked on.

"But you said—" Dad started.

"Here we are," the man said, cutting him off. He stopped in front of a door marked *118*.

"Hey, one eighteen!" Dad said. "Just like your birthday, honey!"

"Right," I said. "January eighteenth. Weird."

"Boooo!" Jason said, waggling his fingers at me.

The innkeeper pulled out a key and opened the door. Then he bowed to welcome us in, dropping the key into Dad's hand as we stepped inside.

"Wow," Jason said. "It's huge."

It was—way bigger than the suite we usually got at the Lakeview. There was a kitchenette just inside the door. The living room sprawled. A fireplace—with a fire already burning—sat nestled in a sunken seating area. Beyond that, a sliding door led out to a private deck.

The three doors—two on one wall, and the third on another—were the bedrooms.

Maybe this place would be better than the Lakeview Inn.

"I'm sure everything will be to your liking," the man said. He was about to leave, and then stopped in the doorway. "I nearly forgot."

He walked right up to me where I stood in the middle of the living room. "Young lady," he said. He grinned, and I had never seen anything so ghastly in all my life. He had all his teeth, but they were too big, too yellow, and chipped and cracked like sun-baked bones in Death Valley.

"I was especially pleased to learn *you'd* be staying here," he went on.

I took two steps back and stumbled into the sunken seating area. Jason caught me by the shoulders.

"M-me?" I said.

"Come with me," he said, and gestured with one long, crooked finger to follow him.

I glanced at Jason, and he got the hint and went with me to follow the old man into one of the bedrooms.

"It's the perfect bedroom for you, don't you think?" the man said, standing in the open doorway.

I stepped inside with Jason's hand in mine and gasped.

My room was lined with shelves, three high on three walls, and the shelves were full of staring, glass-eyed dolls.

My breath caught in my throat. I held tightly to Jason's arm to stop myself from falling over.

The innkeeper smiled at me, his face stretching into a monstrous grin. "I knew you'd like it," he said in a raspy whisper.

"If she's quite keen on any of them," he added louder to our parents in the living room, "they're for sale, prices as marked!"

Leaving me and Jason in the bedroom, he stepped past us, taking one of my hands in his.

He patted it gently. "I'm so pleased to have a little girl staying here," he said. "A guest who might appreciate our little collection."

Little girl? I thought angrily. *I'm thirteen!*

3

"I think you got the biggest room," Jason said.
"Lucky." He left me alone sitting on the double bed
with fifty dolls staring at me.

"I don't feel very lucky," I muttered when he
was out of earshot.

I should probably explain. See, my brother didn't
know—and neither did my parents—but I was
terrified of dolls.

Maybe I didn't even know yet, not really.

Because I played with fashion dolls as a kid, and
with princesses from my favorite movies. But the

dolls in this room at Devil's Mooring scared me to pieces. These were the kind that seemed older than my grandparents. They wore realistic clothes, like a baby might have worn two hundred years ago.

Their painted lips curved in slight smiles. It made them look mean.

Their round cheeks glowed pale pink, so they looked almost alive.

And their eyes. Their glass eyes shined, reflecting the light from the fixture over the bed. The light flickered as the ceiling fan turned slowly.

As the light flickered, their eyes seemed to shift in their heads.

I jumped up from the bed and ran from the room.

"What's your problem?" Jason said as I nearly knocked him down.

"Switch with me," I said, nodding backward toward the doll room.

"No way," Jason said. "It's way too girly for me. You heard the innkeeper."

"Don't be ridiculous," I said. "That's such an outdated way to think."

"It doesn't matter anyway," Jason said, walking away. "I've already mostly unpacked in *my* room. And my room has a TV."

"What?" I said, almost forgetting the creepy dolls. "Jason gets a TV?"

Mom rolled her eyes.

"A TV that gets one channel," Dad said with a playful smile. "The public-access station from town."

"I'm sure Jason will enjoy watching the panel of locals discussing the migratory fish of Lake Superior," Mom joked.

Jason took a moment to glare at the rest of us before retreating into his room and closing the door.

"What about you two?" I said. "Want to switch rooms with me?"

"What?" Mom said. "Why would we do that? Ours has a bathroom."

"And we've already unpacked," Dad added.

"But—," I started to say, but I couldn't bring myself to admit I was afraid of the dolls.

Instead I said, "The dolls are so childish."

"Honey," Mom said, putting a hand on my cheek, "*you* are a child. I think the doll room is sweet. And if you want to pick out your favorite, maybe one will make a nice souvenir for you!"

"Ugh," I said, pulling away. I went into the doll room and closed the door.

I lay on the bed and stared at the ceiling fan, forcing myself not to even glance at the glassy-eyed little creeps surrounding me.

Before long, the fan's lazy spin lulled me to drowsiness. I rolled onto my side, thinking I might catch a quick nap before dinner.

But on my side, all I could see were shelves of dolls. This one, with dark and curly hair tied in a dozen red ribbons. That one, with straight white hair, as fine as spun sugar.

Another, a boy—his hair brown and sticking out in shaggy locks from beneath a blue cap.

And the one that moved: a girl in a green dress with puffs at the shoulders. She had eyes to match her dress and a thousand dark freckles. Her strawberry hair was frizzy and needed a comb.

That girl climbed down from her shelf and crossed the wood floor, but I couldn't move. I could only watch.

She scaled the big bed, a little dollish mountain climber, and she wrapped her tiny wooden hands around my throat.

She began to squeeze. Her glassy eyes flickered. Her sinister smile stretched. I could not breathe. I could not throw her off. I could only stare into her unloving eyes and hear the childish laughter of every doll in the room.

"Wake up, Jas!"

My eyes sprung open. I stared up at the lazily spinning ceiling fan, still on my back.

So I'd fallen asleep.

"What?" I said. Jason stood beside the bed.

"I said wake up, you space case," he said. "It's time to go to dinner."

4

At Tom and Bob's Pizza in town, I sat in the corner of the booth and stared out the restaurant's front windows.

It was a cloudy afternoon. The overcast sky reflected in the great lake so everything from the rocky beach to the horizon and beyond was slate gray and sad looking.

I hardly touched my pizza.

"We probably won't come here again this trip, Jas," Mom said, leaning across the table. "You look forward to Tom and Bob's every year."

I picked up a slice of pizza and took a little bite. It was already cold. The sausage seemed bland, the cheese rubbery.

"I'm not very hungry," I said.

Jason immediately reached over from next to me and snagged one of my slices.

"You can finish it," I said. "I don't care."

Jason looked at me, eyes wide, for a moment. Then he shrugged and grabbed three more slices.

When Jason had stuffed himself completely, we headed down to the walkway along the beach. He and Dad started skipping rocks. Mom perched on a boulder and enjoyed the good cell reception in town, since we'd had none at the inn.

I decided to take a walk on my own.

"Don't go too far!" Mom called after me.

I was almost at the walkway out to the lighthouse when I came upon a boy about my age. He was crouched on the beach building a tower of small, flattish stones. That was a thing visitors liked to do on the lake shore. A tradition, kind of.

I stopped nearby and watched him add stones to the tower. He was very careful. After a few minutes and a few stones, he sat back and said, "Hi."

"Hi," I said. Behind him and west of town, the clouds were breaking up a little. I could see the sunset.

"Arc you staying at the Lakeview too?" he asked.

I shook my head. "They didn't have room for us," I said. "We're staying at a place called Devil's Mooring up the shore a little."

"I've never heard of it," he said, going back to selecting flat rocks for his tower.

I turned to face the lake and squinted into the distance. "You can just see it from here," I said, pointing to a little speck of rusty red near the water, far away.

The boy came up beside me and tried to follow my finger.

"I don't see it at all," he said. Then he turned to

the walkway and called to the old woman sitting on a bench nearby. "Great-grandma, do you know the place Devil's Mooring?"

The woman got up from her bench and walked carefully over the rocky ground to stand with us. "Devil's what?" she asked. "Who's your friend?"

"I'm Jasmine," I said, putting out my hand to shake.

She took my hand and patted it gently, looking into my eyes sincerely. "Aren't you a doll," she said.

"Devil's *Mooring*," the boy repeated.

His great-grandmother stared thoughtfully over the lake. "I *do* remember that place," she finally said.

"Great-grandma lived here for years," the boy explained. "She moved down to the cities when it got too hard for her to drive down to visit all the time."

"I think it closed down in the 1960s," the old woman went on.

"Oh, no," I said. "We're staying there. It's definitely still open."

But the boy's great-grandmother didn't seem to hear me. "The owner of that place, or maybe it was his wife," she went on as she strolled slowly toward the gentle surf, "handmade the most lovely dolls. I think I bought one as a very little girl."

"They still have them," I said.

"Such beautiful dolls," the old woman said, her voice faraway and somehow both sad and happy at once.

"We'd better get back to the inn, Great-grandma," the boy said as he took her by one arm.

Without another word, the boy and the old woman walked off toward the Lakeview.

5

Back at the Devil's Mooring Inn, Mom and Dad settled on the couch to watch a movie. I ushered Jason into his room and closed the door.

"What are you doing?" he said, annoyed.

"Have you noticed anything weird about this place?" I asked, sitting on the edge of the bed.

Jason dropped to the floor to do his push-ups. He did like fifty every night.

"Weird?" he said between puffed breaths. "Besides the dude who runs the place?"

"No, him too," I said.

"And the name?" Jason said, huffing through another push-up. "And the fact that clearly no one else is staying here even though it's like the biggest weekend of the summer for trips up north?"

"Yeah, all that," I said.

"Nah, nothing weird about that," Jason said. He rolled onto his side. "What are you getting at, anyway? So it's a weird place. So what?"

"So I met this boy in town after supper," I started.

Of course, Jason couldn't let that go. "Ooh," he said, and he made a bunch of kissy sounds. "Should we tell Mom to start planning the wedding?"

"Shut up," I said. "The point is his great-grandmother was with him. She seemed to think this inn had closed like fifty or sixty years ago."

"So some old lady has a bad memory," he said. "Quick, hand me my phone. I have to send a text to the FBI's supernatural division."

"You're so annoying," I said. I got up to leave.

"Takes one to know one!" he called after me.

I slammed his door and dropped onto the couch between Mom and Dad.

When the movie ended and the credits were scrolling up the screen, Mom yawned. "Time for you to get to bed," she said.

"I'm not tired," I said. The truth was I didn't want to go to bed in that awful bedroom with those awful dolls.

"Well," Dad said, "we are on vacation. And that love story she likes so much is coming on next. With that English guy."

"Let's watch that," I said. I cuddled against my dad.

"Fine, fine," Mom said. "But there will be no sleeping in tomorrow. I want to get in line for doughnuts *and* hit the hiking trail nice and early."

"OK, Mom," I said as the movie started. "No problem."

I *was* tired, and before long, I fell asleep.

I was hardly aware of Dad carrying me to bed. But when I woke up, dozens of cherubic faces

watched me from the shelves. Their glass eyes shined in the pink morning light coming through the windows.

I sat up. Outside, just steps from my window, the innkeeper stood facing the sunrise. In one hand he held a heavy-looking cloth bag.

When he turned around and saw me, I lay back down and covered myself with the blanket.

Knock-knock. "Rise and shine, Jas," Dad called through the door. "Doughnuts wait for no man—nor girl."

I peeked out from under the blanket. The innkeeper was no longer at the window.

I dressed quickly. Before hurrying to join my family, I stopped to look at the dolls. I don't know what came over me, but almost without thinking I knocked every single one of them onto the floor into a pile.

Then I grabbed the blanket from my bed and raised it high, like one of those parachutes from preschool. It fluttered and fell slowly over the piles of little wooden boys and girls.

Just before it covered them in darkness and hid them completely, one of them—she had blond hair in tight curls, a single fat blue ribbon holding back her ringlets—looked at me and sneered.

6

The morning was beautiful. The line for doughnuts was long, but no one minded. The sun was out, and a cool breeze blew in off the lake to ensure it didn't get too hot.

When Mom pulled into the state park at the bottom of the hiking trail, a few fluffy-looking clouds had made their way overhead.

"Nice day for a hike," said the woman at the gate as we paid for admittance. "Might rain later."

I looked up at the beautiful summer sky. It sure didn't look like rain.

"You know what they say about weather at the lake," the woman at the gate said, fixing her crooked eyes on me. "If you don't like the weather, wait a half an hour."

Mom parked the car. Dad put our doughnuts in his pack, and we started to hike.

We were halfway up the three-mile trail when Dad stopped at an overlook. "I think the attendant might have been right," he said.

I stepped up next to him and leaned on the railing. It shook a little, as if it might break.

I could see the town from there and the lake beyond. The clouds over the horizon were gray and heavy-looking.

"Is it a storm?" I asked.

"Looks like it," Dad said. "Pretty far off, though. I think we'll have plenty of time to finish our hike."

But the woman at the gate must have known more about Great Lakes weather than Dad. Fifteen minutes later, with still almost a mile to go on the hike, the gray clouds had made landfall.

The storm sat just shy of the hillside and seemed to weigh down the sky. I felt I had to duck, as if I might bang my head on the clouds.

I felt the first drop on my cheek. It was big and fat and exploded on my face. "Dad," I said, but a moment later, the skies opened.

"Dad!" I screamed.

"Hurry, hurry!" Mom shouted, pulling her light jacket over her head. She moved quickly up the trail.

Dad ushered me and Jason ahead of him.

I struggled to keep up with Mom. Jason shoved me from behind, hurrying me along.

Quickly the trail was wet—too wet for safe footing. I used the slim trees along the trail like a sideways ladder, but it was no good. My feet slid, and I had to half-crawl and half run.

Jason pushed past me. Dad took my arm and helped me along. Still, we both stumbled and slipped. Before long, we were soaking wet and muddy up to our waists.

We were near the peak. A small log building sat off the trail among the trees. "There!" I shouted over the din of the storm.

Thunder clapped. Dad nodded and whistled with his fingers between his lips.

Jason and Mom turned, and I pointed urgently ahead.

We slipped and tripped up the hill, but we made it. Up close now, I saw the building was older than I realized. It was overgrown with crawling vines. Young trees sprouted from its foundation. Clearly no one had done any groundskeeping here in years.

Jason banged the door open with his shoulder and we all followed him inside. Something scurried. Or several things scurried. Mice, squirrels, raccoons—all of them.

It was dark and musty. An old aluminum table sat in the corner, covered with dust. Against the far wall was a plain-looking desk. An old black phone sat on its top, along with a stack of papers weighed down with a rock.

There was also some old-looking electrical stuff.

"A CB radio," Dad said. He picked up the mouthpiece and clicked the button. Nothing happened. "Wow, this stuff must have been untouched for decades."

He blew on the mouthpiece, and dust puffed off it. He coughed and coughed.

There was a door behind the desk. I checked the knob. It was locked.

"Storage room, probably," Dad said.

I picked up the old phone and put it to my ear. "I think it's dead," I said, replacing the receiver. I wiped the thick dust on my leggings.

Mom wiped off the seat of a faded green vinyl couch. "Well," she said, sitting down with a groan, "if it's been abandoned for fifty years, we can still wait out the storm here, right?"

"For sure," Jason said. He sat next to Mom.

I flipped through the stack of papers on the desk. They were forms of some kind. Each had blank boxes for names and addresses. At the bottom, they asked for credit card information.

In the middle, a larger box asked for "style" and "quantity."

"That's weird," I said aloud.

"What is, honey?" Dad said. He came up next to me and put an arm around my shoulders.

"Well, it looks like whoever stayed in this cabin," I said, "was selling something."

"Huh, that's odd," Dad said. "I just figured—"

"Doughnuts time!" Jason interrupted as he pulled Dad's pack right off his back.

Then the locked door to the storage room flew open.

I screamed.

7

"Whoa, whoa!" said the middle-aged woman who stepped through the door. "Didn't mean to scare you, doll."

She wore a tan and green uniform and a wide-brim hat. A park ranger.

"You just startled us is all," Dad said, forcing a smile. But he was holding me close, and I could hear his heart racing.

"We thought the place was abandoned," Mom said, rising from the couch. She wiped her wet hair off her forehead.

"I hope we're not intruding," Dad added. "Just getting shelter from the storm."

"Oh, of course not," the woman said. "I'm here the whole season. It's nice to have visitors."

"All summer?" I asked. "But . . ."

"Yes?" she said, leaning toward me. She smiled at me, and it seemed eerily familiar. Closer now, I could see that she wore a lot of makeup to hide wrinkles and freckles. Her hair was also dyed to hide the gray. The roots were unmistakable.

"It's just that it's so dusty," I said.

"Jasmine!" Mom snapped. "That is very rude."

The woman laughed. "Oh, I don't mind one bit," she said. She put a hand on my shoulder. It felt cold. "When you live alone and don't get any visitors, I suppose you let a few things go."

"Do you know Devil's Mooring?" I blurted out. I didn't mean to. I just suddenly had to ask.

"The inn?" the park ranger said. "Of course. The owners are friends of mine. Whenever I get down from this mountain, I always stop by for lunch or dinner. Sometimes even a night in one of their rooms with a view of the lake."

I felt relieved. The run-in with that boy and his great-grandmother had me thinking our inn was in some other dimension, an upside-down world with evil dolls. At least the park ranger had heard of it.

Still, the relief didn't last. The nagging worry in my chest faded only for a moment. Then, looking into the park ranger's deep-set eyes, it came back ten-fold.

"Is there a bathroom I can use?" I asked.

"Sure," the woman said. She pulled open the door she'd come out of. "It's just through here."

I looked in. Beyond the doorway it was pitch dark. If there was a door to the bathroom on the far side of the room, I sure couldn't see it.

"Thanks," I said, stepping slowly and blindly into the room. I reached out my hands in front of me as I went, hoping not to knock anything over.

But my foot caught the edge of a table, and I went sprawling. So did the table. We landed with a crash, and the light flicked on.

The park ranger and my dad stood in the doorway behind me. I lay in the middle of the room, a tall pedestal table on the floor beside me.

I pushed myself up and turned my head. On my other side lay something that had fallen off the table: a doll.

I jumped to my feet and spun. The small living room was lined with shelves just like back at the inn, and the shelves were lined with dolls.

A boy there, in a sailor suit. There, a girl, her skin dark and her eyes bright. Beside her, slightly larger, a joyful-looking man with a mustache that twirled from his lips. And next to him, a woman in a fine-looking green dress, her hair set in curls on her head and her hands set primly in her lap.

There were freckles, glasses, beards, purses, winter coats and summer suits, swimming trunks and a set of tiny skis and poles.

I burst from the back room, shoved past the park ranger and my dad, and ran from the old building and into the woods.

8

The rain had all but stopped, but the ground was wet. Fallen leaves and rotted wood and sprouting mushrooms made the ground impossibly slippery, but I couldn't stop.

I slid my way between trees, unable to find the actual path. It was dangerous. It was stupid. But I didn't care. I would risk my life to get as far away from those dolls—and from that woman—as I could, as quickly as I could.

I stumbled along, slowing my descent by getting my hands on as many narrow trees as I could as I went.

My leggings tore. My socks were drenched inside my boots. As the hillside grew steeper, I couldn't slow myself. My legs seemed to fly on their own.

In front of me was wide-open space. I was about to launch off the mountain.

I slammed into the railing at the overlook, the same place I'd stood with my father less than an hour ago. The railing bent and snapped.

9

The railing dangled, barely attached to its cement footing above me. I dangled over the abyss. I couldn't look down.

With one hand, I held tight to the metal bar. With the other, I struggled to reach up to grab hold of the cement and pull myself to safety.

But as I reached, the metal railing screeched in protest and snapped.

I fell. My hands swung wildly, grabbing for any hold. I snapped branches. I knocked against a tree trunk as my feet scrambled on the steep ground, unable to find a perch.

I tumbled and rolled and slammed into a fat old tree stump. I would have fallen farther if I hadn't wrapped my arms around it in a desperate hug.

"Jasmine!" Mom screamed from high above me. "Jasmine, please answer!"

"I'm OK!" I said, my voice wet and too quiet.

"I think I'm OK!" I added, a little louder.

"Stay there," Dad called down to me. "We're coming for you."

"No, I'm OK!" I shouted back.

It was mostly true. I'd have bruises for sure. And my legs were bleeding a little where my leggings had ripped. But I could walk. I got my footing and made my way back to the trail. It was flatter there, and even beginning to dry.

I knew my family was hurrying down to reach me, but I didn't wait. I jogged the rest of the way to the car and leaned on the door.

It was familiar and clean. I laid my forehead on the backseat window and closed my eyes to catch my breath and try to calm down.

"Jasmine!" Dad shouted.

I didn't lift my head till he was at the car with his arms around me. I turned around then and found I was crying.

Back at the inn, I dragged my feet across the lobby.

"My goodness," the old innkeeper said. "What happened to you folks?"

I didn't answer.

"Just got caught in some rain," Dad said. I could hear the phony smile in his voice.

Mom unlocked our suite. I sleepily made my way to my room, pleased I'd find the shelves empty and those wicked creations in a heap under a blanket.

But that's not what I found at all. All the dolls were back in their places. The blond-haired girl with perfect ringlets and a blue ribbon sat in the center of the shelf on the far wall.

"Nice try," she said.

I screamed and ran from the room.

When Mom grabbed me as I ran through the living room, I screamed and tried to get away. Maybe it was her eyes. They're dark brown, and I think for an instant they seemed like glass, like a doll's eyes.

I saw my reflection in Mom's eyes, wide with fear for my safety, and in the reflection, even I looked wrong—like a doll, made of wood, with round cheeks tinted pink.

She led me to the couch and laid me down. Dad put a pillow under my head.

"I'm sorry," I said, barely a whisper. It was all I had strength for. "I should have told you I was terrified in there."

"In where, dear?" Mom said.

I looked toward my bedroom. "The dolls," I said. "They hate me. I mean, I hate them."

Dad sat on the coffee table. Mom went to the phone on the end table and dialed the front desk.

"No one's picking up," Mom said. "This place."

"All right, let's all try to calm down," Dad said. "I'm sure they can put us in a different suite. If not, certainly Jason won't mind switching rooms for the next couple of nights."

"What?!" Jason said. "No way. I—"

Dad and Mom glared at him.

"Fine, fine," Jason said. "Anything for my crazy little sister, right?"

He slapped my foot and winked at me.

There came a knock at the door.

"Everything all right in there?" the innkeeper said from the hallway.

"Good," Mom said, rising from the couch beside me. "I'll get us a new suite right now."

Mom opened the door, and the old man came in. He spotted me at once and limped toward me. "Is she ill?" he asked. He didn't look worried. Not exactly. Instead he looked . . . disappointed.

"She'll be fine," Mom said. "But we would really like to be moved to a different suite."

"Can't be done," the innkeeper said before Mom could even explain. "No vacancies. We're full up."

"Full up?" Jason said. "Is he kidding?"

The old man sneered at Jason and fixed him with a cockeyed glare.

"We haven't seen another soul in the inn since we've been here," Dad said. "Not in the lobby, not on the beach, not in the lot out front."

"Oh, plenty of souls here," the innkeeper said. He chuckled at his own joke, if that's what it had been.

He gave me another long and curious look before turning to leave. "Oh, I nearly forgot why I came down here," he said in the doorway as he turned around. "The dolls in your room, little girl."

My heart thumped. "What about them?" I asked.

"My wife was cleaning while you folks were on your hike," he said. "She found all the dolls in a heap on the floor."

"Oh," I said, now truly relieved.

"Mustn't do that again," he added, his voice stern and his chin high in authority. "They're not for playing with unless you plan to buy 'em."

"Sorry," I said. "I won't do that again."

He nodded, turned, and left, closing the door behind him.

10

We had a quiet afternoon. Jason got all my stuff out of the doll room and brought it into his room.

"Thanks, Jace," I said from the couch, smiling up at him. He could be a real monster sometimes, but he was often so sweet. A real doll.

"No problem," he said as he hopped over the arm of the couch and sat by my feet. "Anything on TV?"

"You don't have to hang out with me just because I'm bonkers," I said. "Go enjoy the lake!"

But Jason ignored me. When Mom and Dad went into town to buy groceries for dinner on the patio, he and I just sat in front of the TV for a couple of hours.

Jason let me doze. When I woke up, he made me some tea. When a baseball game came on and I groaned, he put on a drama series on a different channel for me.

It was so strange. My parents and my brother now knew how I felt about those dolls. But they hadn't laughed at me. Even Jason was being amazing.

I was sure the rest of the vacation would be great, once I got some rest after the morning's adventure.

"Who wants a burger?" Dad said happily as he and Mom came into the suite, laden with paper bags. "I got burgers, hot dogs, bacon, chips, guacamole—"

"We bought half the store," Mom said, cutting him off with a sly smile. "And fear not: we've plenty of ice cream for dessert."

"Strawberry?" I said, sitting up a little.

Mom held up the pink pint. "Do I know my little girl?" she said.

"Thanks, Mom," I said. Everyone was being amazing.

Dad and Jason went out on the deck to start the coals for the grill. Mom sat on the loveseat next to the couch and read a magazine.

I fell asleep.

When I woke, it was dark in the living room. Mom wasn't on the loveseat with her magazine. I had that unsettling feeling of having napped until after sundown, and for a moment I didn't know where I was, or what time of day it was. But I could smell burgers through the screen door to the patio.

The TV was still on, showing a crime show from twenty years ago. Two men in overcoats asked a third man in a hoodie where he was on the night of the fifteenth.

The TV turned off with a strange sucking sound. It was quiet. Even the fridge stopped humming.

Power's out, I thought. I sat up. "Mom?" I called. No one answered.

I stood up. My legs were a bit wobbly—maybe from lying around all afternoon, or maybe from my express trip down the cliffside.

"Dad? Jace?" I said through the screen door. But outside it was even darker. I could hear the lake, though, sloshing onto the rocks of the beach. It was a beautiful sound.

It would soon grow to be interminable.

"Maybe everyone went to bed already," I muttered to myself. "Maybe I slept through dinner."

I pulled the sliding door closed, quieting the lake a bit. The lulling *whoosh* still found its way inside through the open windows.

A single light glowed under the door to my bedroom. Jason's bedroom now, of course.

But if the power's out, I thought, *why is there a light on in there?*

"A book light," I whispered to myself. "Jason probably brought one from home, battery operated."

I knocked gently on the door, hoping to see my brother's comforting face in a moment. But he didn't answer.

I turned the knob quietly and opened the door. The bed was empty. The light came from the fixture, where the fan spun lazily.

"There she is," said the blond girl with the ringlets and the blue ribbon. "We've waited all afternoon, you know."

"Jason!" I screamed. "Mom! Dad! Where are you?!"

I turned from the doll room and ran for the door to the suite. I grabbed the doorknob and tugged at it madly. The door was locked.

I turned the deadbolt. I flicked the little lock set into the knob. The door would not budge.

The patio, I thought, and I started across the living room. But before I passed the door to the doll room, it opened again. Light poured into the living room, and with a horde of those fiendish, tiny boys and girls.

"There's nothing to be afraid of, Jasmine," said one of the dolls. He was tall, and looked a bit stronger than the others. He had a wry smile. I almost found his face comforting.

"Jason?" I said.

I ran to the kitchen and grabbed a broom. As the dolls moved closer, I swung it wildly, knocking a few against the wall. One little wooden arm knocked loose. Another lost her red ribbon.

"Jasmine, darling," said my mother's voice. I found her face—big brown eyes, tiny nose set between high, proud cheekbones. "Stop this at once. You're making a scene."

I'm not ashamed to say I screamed then, the loudest I'd ever screamed in my life. But it did no good. I dropped the broom, and the horde of dolls overcame me.

I fell. My head banged hard on the tile floor of the kitchenette, and everything went black.

It's not bad now. It's quiet here, and sometimes I'm facing a window so I can look at the lake. I'm with my family too. Dad's painted-on beard isn't quite right. Mom's glasses have strange frames and no lenses. I suppose she can't see very well. Jason's in a little Sunday suit. It's not his taste at all, and I imagine the two of us laughing about it someday.

We can't laugh though, of course. Our mouths don't work at all.

I just hope when I'm bought—*if* I'm bought—that the buyers take the rest of my family too. I'd hate to sit on a shelf someplace all alone.

GLOSSARY

aluminum (uh-LOO-mi-nuhm)—a type of metal

authority (uh-THOR-uh-tee)—official, or coming from someone who has the power to give orders

dimension (duh-MEN-shuhn)—a different world from our own

drowsiness (DROU-zee-ness)—nearly asleep

flickered (FLIK-urd)—to burn unsteadily or with a constantly changing light

horde (HORD)—a large and unorganized group of individuals

innkeeper (IN-kee-per)—the owner or manager of an inn

interminable (ihn-TUHR-mih-nuh-bul)—to seem endless

kitchenette (kich-uh-NET)—a very small kitchen

rubbery (RUHB-ur-ee)—like rubber in appearance or stretchiness

sun-baked (SUHN-bayked)—dried out, chapped, or cracked by the sun's heat

vacancies (VAY-kuhn-sees)—something (such as hotel rooms) that are empty and not being used

zigzag (ZIG-zag)—to move in short, sharp turns or angles from one side to the other

FACE YOUR FEAR!

Now that you've read the story, it's no longer only inside this book. It's also in your brain. Can your brain help you answer the prompts below?

1. Think about a scary toy you've seen. Did it seem as haunted as the dolls Jasmine found?

2. Imagine a different ending of the story, wherein Jasmine and her family escape the hotel. How do they get away from the innkeeper?

3. What hints were there that something was wrong with the Devil's Mooring hotel? Use examples from the text to discuss the scary signs.

4. Can you explain why the innkeeper is so happy that Jasmine is staying at his hotel? What details in the text support your explanation?

5. Jasmine describes the great-grandmother's voice as "Both sad and happy at once" when she's talking about the dolls. What do you think Jasmine means by this?

FEAR FACTORS

pediophobia (pee-dee-oh-FOH-bee-uh)—the fear of dolls

Scientists believe that a fear of dolls comes from the "uncanny effect" on the brain. "Uncanny" means "oddly different" or "strangely uncomfortable." At first glance, our brains tell us that dolls are humans. Then the brain realizes something is not quite right. The dolls are not human because they're too small. This jumping back and forth in our brains between real and unreal causes the uncanny effect and can produce uneasiness or fear.

In Thailand, a strange fad is collecting human-size dolls. The elaborately dressed dolls are considered good luck charms. But some people believe that the spirits of young children inhabit the human-like toys.

Voodoo dolls have been a part of folklore from Africa to Europe throughout the centuries. The doll is made to resemble a specific living person. Pins are stuck into the doll, with the superstitious wish that the person it looks like will feel pain in those same parts of the body. These dolls, sometimes called poppets, could be made of clay, sticks, rags, wax, paper, or carved from tree roots.

The town of Nagoro, Japan, is filled with human-size dolls. There are whole classrooms where seats are filled with only doll students. Doll teachers stand in the dark halls. Doll workers hoe and weed nearby fields. Dolls climb trees, sit on front porches, and welcome visitors to their village. In 2003, resident Ayano Tsukimi watched as her town's population grew smaller with people dying or leaving for bigger cities. So Ayano started making life-size replicas of the departed, placing them in locations and poses in memory of their life-size models. Do not visit this town after dark!

ABOUT THE AUTHOR

Steve Brezenoff is the author of more than fifty middle-grade chapter books, including the Field Trip Mysteries series, the Ravens Pass series of thrillers, and the Return to the Titanic series. He's also written three young-adult novels, *Guy in Real Life*; *Brooklyn, Burning*; and *The Absolute Value of -1*. In his spare time, he enjoys video games, cycling, and cooking. Steve lives in Minneapolis with his wife, Beth, and their son and daughter.

ABOUT THE ILLUSTRATOR

Mariano Epelbaum is a character designer, illustrator, and traditional 2D animator. He has been working as a professional artist since 1996, and enjoys trying different art styles and techniques. Throughout his career Mariano has created characters and designs for a wide range of films, TV series, commercials, and publications in his native country of Argentina. In addition to Michael Dahl Presents: Phobia, Mariano has also contributed to the Fairy Tale Mix-ups, You Choose: Fractured Fairy Tales, and Snoops, Inc. series for Capstone.

GRIMM
AND
GROSS

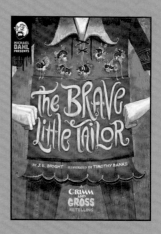

only from capstone